Caillou®

Chinese New Year

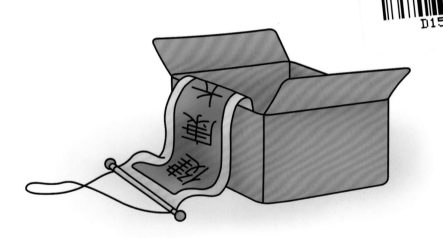

Adaptation from the animated series: Corinne Delporte
Illustrations taken from the animated series and adapted by Mario Allard

Caillou was playing in the snow when he met his friend Sarah with another girl.

"Hi Caillou, this is my cousin Lee-Wun. She is visiting us for Chinese New Year."

Caillou had never heard of it. Sarah explained to Caillou that it was the most popular Chinese festival.

"We're going to celebrate the start of the lunar new year!" said Lee-Wun.

Sarah invited Caillou to her house to show him their Chinese New Year's decorations.

She hung a poster with Chinese characters wishing lots of happiness for the New Year.

Caillou carried a second poster with Lee-Wun.

"And that one is to wish you a healthy long life," explained Sarah.

"Tomorrow, we are going to see a dragon!" said Sarah. Caillou was surprised. He could hardly believe that dragons existed. Lee-Wun invited him to come with them. Caillou hesitated. He was a bit scared to see a real dragon. But he was also very curious. He finally decided he wanted to go.

Sarah's mom came into the room.
"Caillou would like to see the dragon tomorrow,"
said Sarah.
"That's great! I'll give Caillou's mom a call to ask
if we can take him to Chinatown."

"Don't forget to clean your room, girls!" said Sarah's mom.
Sarah told Caillou it was part of the New Year tradition to clean the house from top to bottom.
"Why?" asked Caillou.
"To bring good luck to the family," Sarah said.

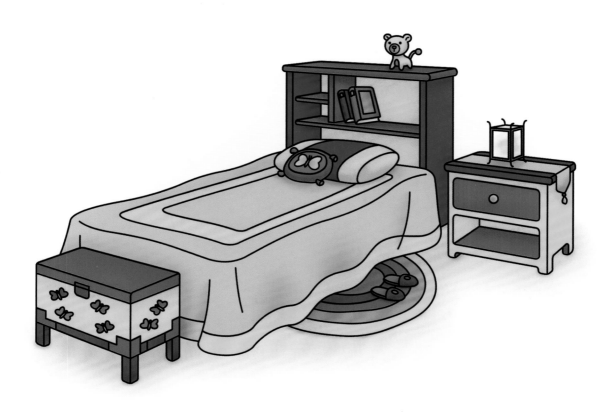

"Speaking of good luck, did you get a special New Year coin?" asked Lee-Wun.

Caillou hadn't. The two girls felt sorry for him. They gave Caillou a New Year coin in a beautiful red envelope. Caillou was happy. He had never seen a New Year coin before.

When Caillou went to bed that night, he was excited but also a bit nervous about seeing a dragon. He wasn't sure he wanted to go anymore.

Mom wanted to help him feel better, so she read Caillou the story about the big friendly dragon. Caillou was very happy. It was one of his favorite stories.

The next day, Caillou and his friends went to Chinatown to eat a special New Year's meal. Sarah and Lee-Wun showed Caillou something interesting about the table: there was a rotating tray in the middle for the food. Caillou really wanted to try it.

When Sarah's dad asked them to pass the dumplings, Caillou and Sarah made the tray turn around until the dumplings came back to them. They giggled and Sarah gave Caillou a dumpling with her chopsticks. Caillou was having a lot of fun. He enjoyed tasting all the new foods.

It was hard for Caillou to use the chopsticks, so Sarah helped him.
"You can use a spoon to eat the *Tangyuan!* It is a Chinese sweet," said Lee-Wun.
Caillou was happy: it was much easier that way!
"It's delicious," he said as he gobbled up one after another.

Suddenly, Caillou heard music and clapping.
"The dragon is coming!" said Sarah excitedly.
The dragon came into the restaurant. It was not scary
at all! Caillou loved seeing it.
"Happy New Year!" cheered Caillou and his friends.

Xin Nian Kuai Le!
Sheen Nian Kwai Luh!

Text: adaptation by Corinne Delporte of the animated series CAILLOU,
produced by DHX Media Inc.
All rights reserved.
Original story: Matthew Cope
Original episode #83 Happy New Year
Illustrations: Mario Allard, based on the animated series CAILLOU
Coloration: Eric Lehouillier

The PBS KIDS logo is a registered mark of PBS and is used with permission.

Chouette Publishing would like to thank the Government of Canada and SODEC
for their financial support.

Books
Tax Credit

Gestion
SODEC

Bibliothèque et Archives nationales du Québec and Library and Archives
Canada cataloguing in publication

Delporte, Corinne, author

Caillou, Chinese New Year: dragon mask and mosaic stickers included/text,
Corinne Delporte; illustrations, Mario Allard.

(Playtime)

Target audience: For children aged 3 and up.

ISBN 978-2-89718-498-8 (softcover)

1. Chinese New Year - Juvenile literature. I. Allard, Mario, 1969-, illustrator.
II. Title. III. Series: Playtime (Montréal, Québec).

GT4905.D44 2018   j394.26   C2018-940484-1

Printed in China
10 9 8 7 6 5 4 3 2 1 CHO2033 MAY2018

MAKE YOUR OWN DRAGON MASK!

Instructions: Color the mask. Turn it around and use stickers in matching shapes and colors to decorate the mask.

Ask an adult to help you cut the mask, cut the holes and thread a piece of elastic through.